The King with Dirty Feet

and Other Stories from Around the World

Compiled by Mary Medlicott

Illustrated by Sue Williams

KINGFISHER

NEW YORK

For Tom and David M.M.
For my mother, Patricia Williams S.W.

KINGFISHER
Larousse Kingfisher Chambers Inc.
95 Madison Avenue
New York, New York 10016

This paperback edition first published in the U.S. by Kingfisher 1998
2 4 6 8 10 9 7 5 3 1

Material in this edition was originally published in hardcover
in the U.S. by Kingfisher in 1992 in *Tales for Telling*

LIBRARY OF CONGRESS CATALOGING-IN-PUBLICATION DATA
The King with dirty feet and other stories from around the world/compiled by Mary
Medlicott; illustrated by Sue Williams.
p.   cm.
Contents: The king with dirty feet/P. Clayton—Clever Rabbit
and King Lion/A. Kwapong—Cherry Tree Hill/H. East—The
Hedley kow/M. Pearson—The great rain/L. Cotterill.
1. Tales. [1. Folklore.] I. Williams, Sue. ill.
PZ8.1.K612   1999
398.2—dc21   97-47591
CIP   AC

ISBN 0-7534-5165-4
Printed in Hong Kong / China

CONTENTS

The King With Dirty Feet

A tale from India

•

Pomme Clayton

Once upon a time, there was a king. He lived in a hot, dusty village in India. He had everything he wanted and was very happy. But there was one thing that this king hated and that was bathtime.

Perhaps he was a little bit like you?

This king had not washed for a week; he had not washed for a month; he had not washed for a whole year. He had begun to smell. He smelled underneath his arms, in between his toes, behind his ears, and up his nose. He was the smelliest king there has ever been. His servants were all very polite about it, but nobody liked to be in the same room as him. Until one day the smell became too much for even the king himself, and he said rather sadly, "I think it is time I had a bath."

He walked slowly down to the river. The villagers whispered, "The king's going to have a bath!," and they rushed down to the river bank to get the best view.

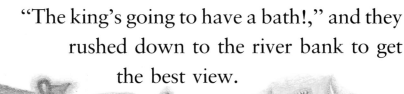

Everyone fell silent when the king stepped into the cool, clear river water. When he called for the royal soap, a huge cheer arose. He washed himself from top to bottom, scrubbed his hair, and brushed his teeth. He played with his toy ducks and his little boat.

Then, at last, when he was quite clean, he called for the royal towel and stepped out of the river.

When he had finished drying himself, he saw that his feet were covered with dust.

"Oh, bother," he cried. "I forgot to wash them." So he stepped back into the water and soaped them well. But as soon as he stood on dry land, his feet were dirty again.

"Oh, my goodness," he said crossly. "I didn't wash them well enough. Bring me a scrubbing brush." The king scrubbed his feet until they shone. But still, when he stepped on the ground, they were dirty.

This time, the king was furious. He shouted for his servant, Gabu. Gabu came running and bowed low before the king.

"Gabu," boomed the king, "the king has had a bath, the king is clean, but the earth is dirty. There is dust everywhere. You must clean the earth so there is no more dust and my feet stay clean."

"Yes, Your Majesty," replied Gabu.

"You have three days in which to rid the land of dust, and if you fail, do you know what will happen to you?" asked the king.

"No, Your Majesty."

"ZUT!" cried the king.

"ZUT?" said Gabu. "What is ZUT?"

"ZUT is the sound of your head being chopped off."

Gabu began to cry.

"Don't waste time, Gabu. Rid the land of dust at once."

The king marched back to his palace.

"I must put my thinking cap on," said Gabu, and he put his head in his hands and began to think.

"When something is dirty, you brush it."

He asked all the villagers to help him. They took their brushes and brooms and ONE...TWO...THREE...

They all began to sweep – swish, swish, swish, swish, swish – all day long.

The dust rose up and filled the air in a thick, dark cloud. Everyone was coughing and spluttering and bumping into each other. The king choked, "Gabu, where are you? I asked you to rid the land of dust, not fill the air with it. Gabu, you have two more days and ZUT!"

"Oh dear, oh dear," cried Gabu, and put his head in his hands and thought.

"When something is dirty, you wash it."

He asked all the villagers to help him. They took their buckets to the well and filled them up to the brim with water and ONE...TWO...THREE...

They all began to pour – sloosh, sloosh, sloosh, sloosh, sloosh – all day long.

There was so much water it spread across the land. It began to rise. Soon it was up to their ankles, their knees, their waists, and then up to their chests.

"Swim everybody," cried Gabu.

The king climbed to the top of the highest mountain where the water lapped his toes and he sniffed, "Gabu, a...atchoo! Where are you?"

Gabu came swimming.

"Yes, Your Majesty?"

"Gabu, I asked you to rid the land of dust, not turn our village into a swimming pool. You have one more day and ZUT!"

"Oh dear, oh dear, I have run out of ideas," cried Gabu. The water trickled away, and Gabu put his head in his hands and thought.

"I could put the king in an iron room with no windows or doors, chinks or cracks, then no speck of dust could creep in. But I don't think he would like that. Oh, if only I could cover up all the dust with a carpet." Then Gabu had a marvelous idea.

"Of course, why didn't I think of this before? Everyone has a needle and thread and a little piece of leather. Leather is tough; we will cover the land with leather."

He asked all the villagers to help him. Needles were threaded and knots were tied and ONE...TWO...THREE...

They all began to sew – stitch, stitch, stitch, stitch, stitch – all day long.

Then the huge piece of leather was spread across the land, and it fitted perfectly. It stretched from the school to the well, from the temple to the palace, and all the way down to the river.

"We've done it," cried Gabu. "I will go and tell the king."

Gabu knocked on the palace door.

"We are ready, Your Majesty."

The king poked his head carefully around the door not knowing what to expect. Then a little smile twitched at the corners of his mouth. The ground looked clean, very clean indeed. He put one foot on the leather, and it was spotless. The king walked across the leather.

"This is splendid, comfortable, clean. Well done, Gabu. Well done."

The king turned to the villagers to thank them.

Suddenly, out of the crowd stepped a little old man with a long white beard and a bent back. Everyone had quite forgotten him. He bowed low before the king and spoke in a very quiet voice.

"Your Majesty, how will anything be able to grow, now that the land is covered with leather? The grass will not be able to push its way through. There will be no vegetables or flowers, and no new trees. The animals will be hungry, and there will be nothing for us to eat."

Now everyone was listening.

"Your Majesty, you know you don't have to cover the land with leather to keep your feet clean. It is really quite simple."

The old man took out of his pocket a large pair of scissors. He bent down and began to cut the leather very carefully all around the king's feet. Then he took two laces from his pocket and tied each piece of leather to the king's feet. Then he pulled back the leather that covered the earth and said, "Try them, Your Majesty."

The king looked down at his feet covered in leather and frowned. He had never seen anything like it. He put one foot forward.

"Mmm, very good!" he exclaimed. He took another step.

"This is splendid, comfortable, clean, *and* the grass can grow!"

Then the king walked, then he ran, and then he jumped.

"Hooray," he cried. "I can walk here, and here, and here. I can walk anywhere, and my feet will always be clean."

What was the king wearing on his feet?

That's right; he was wearing SHOES!

They were the first pair of shoes ever to be made, and people have been wearing them ever since.

SNIP, SNAP, SNOUT, MY STORY IS OUT!

Clever Rabbit and King Lion

A story from Ghana

•

Amoafi Kwapong

Once upon a time, and a very good time it was, there lived in the rain forest of Ghana many animals, and Lion was their king.

King Lion lived in the best cave on one side of the forest, while the rest of the animals shared the other side. The other animals were not amused, but they had no choice than to remain where they were.

Clever Rabbit was a very close friend of Madam Hare. Clever Rabbit was very quick at solving problems and riddles, which earned her the title of "Clever." Madam Hare was known in the whole wide forest as a kindhearted lady. With her long ears, Madam Hare could hear a long way away.

One day, Madam Hare overheard King Lion talking to his wife. He was boasting about a plan of his to eat up Clever Rabbit. He had already eaten most of the little animals in the forest.

"Today," he said, "it's Clever Rabbit's turn."

Madam Hare was very upset. She hurried to tell Clever Rabbit what she had heard. At first Clever Rabbit was very upset, too. She thought to herself, "I mind my own business, and I don't deserve this." Madam Hare tried to console her, but Clever Rabbit said, "Action is what I need."

Clever Rabbit had a quick think, and she came up with an idea.

"I'll go to King Lion's cave and offer myself to him. I bet he'll be so angry and confused he won't eat me just yet."

"Very good," replied Madam Hare.

Clever Rabbit set out for King Lion's cave.

Meanwhile, King Lion was on his way to Clever Rabbit's burrow. Halfway down the path, King Lion and Clever Rabbit met face to face. King Lion's eyes were red, and he looked fierce. Clever Rabbit put on a brave face and a smile. She greeted King Lion, "Good morning, Your Majesty. I heard you were going to eat me up for dinner today. So I wanted to make it easier for you by offering myself to you."

"Don't be sassy, you little rascal," answered King Lion.

Clever Rabbit continued, "I didn't mean to be sassy, Your Majesty, but on second thought, I don't think you'll enjoy eating me just yet. Give me three weeks to fatten up for you. You see, I'm all bones."

"Very well," retorted King Lion. "I can wait three weeks."

So off went Clever Rabbit to her burrow, stopping on the way to tell Madam Hare the good news. "Hooray! Hooray!" cried the two friends.

A week passed, but Clever Rabbit looked the same. A second week passed, and still Clever Rabbit had not added an ounce of flesh to her skinny body.

After two weeks, King Lion began to count the seconds, the minutes, the hours. Day one came and went. Then it was day two, day three, day four, day five, day six, and day seven!

"Three weeks are up! I'm going to feast on rabbit today!" gloated King Lion.

Clever Rabbit dressed in her prettiest clothes with bows in her hair. On her way to King Lion's cave, she stopped to chat with Madam Hare. Madam Hare wished Clever Rabbit the best of luck saying, "I trust that you'll come back again."

"Thank you," said Clever Rabbit, "I certainly need a lot of luck today." And off she went.

When she arrived at King Lion's cave, King Lion was working up his appetite. He was just about to pounce on Clever Rabbit when she said, "Oh, Your Majesty, you should hear this! There's a *bigger* lion not too far away from here who's been competing with you. He's eating all the little animals there, and I hear he's eaten more than you have."

"Is that so?" said King Lion. "Show me the way to this arrogant lion and I'll soon let him have it."

Clever Rabbit led the way. She was so overjoyed at not being gobbled up by King Lion that she began to sing, dance, and skip along the path. King Lion was not amused. He roared at Clever Rabbit, "Stop singing, dancing, and skipping at once!" Clever Rabbit stopped at once.

Soon they were both standing by a lake. Clever Rabbit pointed to a spot where King Lion should stand and look in the water. King Lion quickly stood on that spot and stretched to look in the water. There was another lion! Quick as a flash, King Lion jumped into the lake to fight the other lion.

Too late, he realized that Clever Rabbit had tricked him! He struggled to get out of the water. But as you and I know, cats (even big cats) can't swim too well. King Lion drowned, and Clever Rabbit was free to sing, dance, and skip again. She sang and danced and skipped all the way back to Madam Hare who was waiting anxiously.

Clever Rabbit and Madam Hare sang, danced, and skipped together all night long. And when the other little animals of the rain forest heard what had happened, they hurried to join in the celebration.

The story that you've just heard, take it with you and share it.

Cherry Tree Hill

An Australian settlers' yarn

•

Helen East

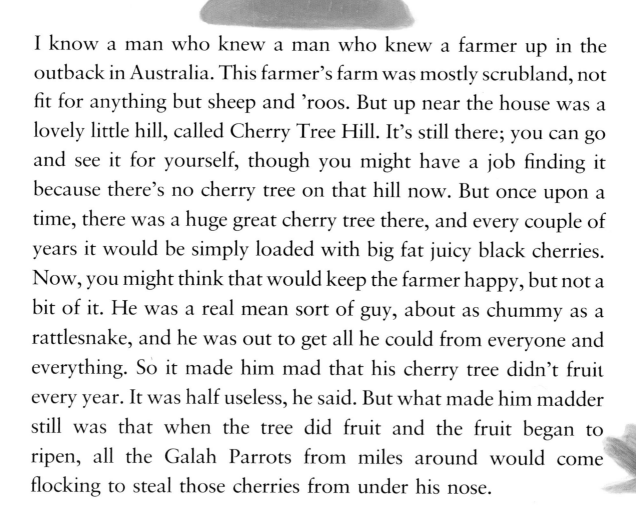

I know a man who knew a man who knew a farmer up in the outback in Australia. This farmer's farm was mostly scrubland, not fit for anything but sheep and 'roos. But up near the house was a lovely little hill, called Cherry Tree Hill. It's still there; you can go and see it for yourself, though you might have a job finding it because there's no cherry tree on that hill now. But once upon a time, there was a huge great cherry tree there, and every couple of years it would be simply loaded with big fat juicy black cherries. Now, you might think that would keep the farmer happy, but not a bit of it. He was a real mean sort of guy, about as chummy as a rattlesnake, and he was out to get all he could from everyone and everything. So it made him mad that his cherry tree didn't fruit every year. It was half useless, he said. But what made him madder still was that when the tree did fruit and the fruit began to ripen, all the Galah Parrots from miles around would come flocking to steal those cherries from under his nose.

He'd try everything to scare them off—scarecrows, jangling cans, nets, wires, the works. He even had his little son out morning, noon, and night, trying to knock those birds down with his slingshot. "Dollar a dozen dead'uns," the farmer promised, but his son never got even a penny, for those Galahs were harder to catch than the Devil himself. They would wait till the boy was almost on them, and then they would sidestep or swing or simply flap to safety, shrieking with raucous laughter. And the farmer got madder than mad just watching them.

So now one year he said to his wife, "This time those Galahs are gonna get it, 'cause this time I'll dang well give it to 'em meself!"

And he took his gun and parked himself right under that tree and he waited. Well, he waited one day, two days, three days, and he waited one night, two nights, three nights, but all he got was a stiff neck, a sore head, and a worse temper. Those Galahs had spotted him from miles away, and they just kept a safe distance and bided their time.

"Drat those darn Galahs!" the farmer snarled as he

stamped off home for a drink and a think. And then, out of the blue, it just came to him. A real dingo of a plan! A way to get the whole bunch at once – and it couldn't fail! For the first time in years, the farmer grinned. He went back to the house, got out his truck and drove the eighty miles to the nearest town. When he got back, he had a great big barrel up on the seat beside him, and he was still grinning. But he wouldn't let on to anyone what was up. He just bided his time, watched the Galahs flocking around the tree, and grinned till you'd think his face would split.

Well, that night, when everyone else was asleep, the farmer got the barrel out and rolled it up the hill. As soon as he got near the tree, the Galahs, asleep on the branches, woke up and flew quickly out of reach. But the farmer didn't care. He just opened up his barrel, picked up a paintbrush, dipped it in, and began to paint that cherry tree, very carefully, all over, from the top down to the bottom. And when every branch and every twig and every leaf was covered, the farmer threw away the empty barrel, washed his hands, and went home to bed.

As soon as the farmer was safely gone, the roosting Galahs returned to the tree. When dawn came, their friends and relatives came to join them for breakfast, and as the morning wore on, latecomers from more distant parts arrived in cheery, cackling crowds. Yet still the farmer slept on. By the time he finally woke up, around noon, the tree was so laden with birds you could hardly see the cherries, and the farmer's family had given up hoping for any fruit at all that year. But the farmer just grinned and loaded his gun.

"I said I'd get them Galahs, and I'm gonna get them good!" he said. And out he went, with his son at his heels.

Well, the Galahs saw them coming, of course, but they weren't worried. They had plenty of time to finish feasting before the farmer got too close. It wasn't until he was halfway up the hill that one old bird roused herself and gave the call to the others. "Better move along, boys," and she lazily flapped her wings.

But, oh! What was this? Her wings moved, but her feet stayed right where they were, held fast to the branch. For do you know what the farmer had painted that cherry tree with so carefully? Glue! The stickiest, stretchiest, strongest glue you ever could imagine. And of course, those Galahs had settled right on it, and now they were stuck tight.

And the farmer thought it was the funniest sight he had ever seen. The harder those birds flapped, and the louder they squawked, the more he liked it. He was laughing so much he could hardly aim his gun. Bang! His first shot went right up into the air. Didn't so much as graze one wing, but it put the Galahs into even more of a panic. And they flapped so wildly the wind whistled through the leaves, and the cherries were blown this way and that, and the branches were weaving and crashing and thrashing. And they flapped so frantically the tree itself began to sway and to swirl and to turn and to lift until, with a tremendous tearing roar, the roots were ripped right out of the ground, and the tree rose into the air. Up! Up! Up! Carried by the beating wings of a thousand grateful Galahs.

As for the farmer and his son, they were so astonished they were rooted to the spot, gawping goggle-eyed, till the birds and their burden were no more than a speck in the sky. And all that was left of the cherry tree was the name of the hill and a darn great gaping hole.

But as for the Galahs, some people say that they are flying to this day. So next time you think you see a plane – rub your eyes and look again.

How Turtle Lost Her Sandals

An Amerindian legend from Guyana

•

Grace Nichols

Once upon a long ago time, Turtle was one of the fastest animals in all the land, though you wouldn't believe it by looking at her now, moving around like a slow-coach. Well, Turtle was fast in those days because, you see, she had two fine pairs of hoofs which took her wherever she wanted to go in no time, even though her legs were short. Turtle was very proud of her beautiful hoofs, which she used to call "my sandals."

Now, a lot of animals were jealous of Turtle and her sandals, but one animal who was really really jealous of Turtle was Deer. Yes, Deer, my dear children. Deer was very slow in that long ago time because she had claws at the end of her feet instead of hoofs, and she moved about in a slow clumsy fashion.

Oh, many a day you could see Deer admiring her antlers in a stream, but whenever she looked down at her feet, she would get annoyed and think, "If only I had fast hoofs like that stupid low-down Turtle to run like a fire through the forest." The more Deer thought about Turtle's beautiful hoofs, the more jealous she became until one day she thought of a plan to get Turtle's hoofs.

It was a hot sunny morning, and Turtle was resting under the shade of a big tree when who should come up to her?

"Good morning, Turtle," Deer said in her sweetest voice.

"Oh, good morning, Deer," said turtle, who was really surprised since Deer had never stopped to talk to her before.

"It's a fine morning," Deer said, brightly.

"Yes," replied Turtle, beginning to wonder what Deer really wanted. Nearly every morning was fine in their part of the world.

After a little pause, Deer looked down at Turtle's hoofs as if she was seeing them for the first time.

"What a beautiful pair of sandals you have," she exclaimed.

"Yes, they're lovely, even though I say so myself," agreed Turtle, feeling nice that someone liked her sandals.

Then Deer put on her most pleading voice and said, "Oh, Turtle, please let me have a try of your sandals. It will give me such pleasure to move quickly for a change. You can't imagine what it's like crawling around all the time, and I would be back before you could even call my name."

"Please, Turtle," Deer begged again, "just for a minute."

Turtle didn't like parting with her precious sandals, but she felt sorry for Deer, and after a while she bent down to unclip them.

"Please bring them back quickly," she said, handing over her sandal-hoofs.

Deer put them on quickly. She ran like the fire. She ran like the wind. Deer was so delighted with the sandals that she decided she was never going to give them back to Turtle.

Meanwhile, Turtle waited on Deer to return her beautiful sandals. She waited and she waited and she waited. After many days of waiting, Turtle knew that Deer wasn't going to return her sandals. At long last, Turtle did the only thing she could do. Slowly she fitted on the claws that Deer had left behind.

But it is said that from that day to today Turtle is still hoping that Deer will bring back her sandals. And while Deer runs like the fire and the wind through the forest, poor Turtle crawls about ever so slow, poking her head out at times, listening and waiting, listening and waiting.

The Hedley Kow

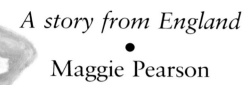

A story from England

●

Maggie Pearson

What sort of creature is the Hedley Kow? It's not a cow, that's for sure – well, only sometimes. Sometimes it looks like a cow.

Sometimes like a horse – and a very fine horse, too, until you try to ride it. Then it's likely to turn itself into a bale of straw, or a pool of water, or... You may see the Hedley Kow and never know it: who's to say?

There was an old woman who made ends meet as best she could. A bit of sewing here. A bit of apple-picking there. A bit of mowing in some other place. It was a hard life, but she made the best of it.

One day while she was walking home, she spied what looked like an old cooking pot lying in the ditch.

"Well!" she said. "There's a lucky thing! I daresay the pot has a hole in it, or it wouldn't have been thrown away, but it's just the thing to stand on my windowsill with a pot of flowers inside it." She went and looked at the pot more closely. It was full of gold pieces.

"Well!" she said. "That is a lucky thing! It's a case of finders keepers, I suppose. I shall be able to live in comfort for the rest of my days."

The pot of gold was too heavy to carry, so she tied her shawl around it and began to drag it home.

Even then, it was hard work, and after a while, she had to stop and rest. She looked inside the pot again.

"Well!" she said. "It's not gold after all, it's silver. That's luckier still. I shouldn't have been happy with all that gold about the house. There's thieves and there's beggars and there's the neighbors getting jealous. I'll be much better off with silver."

Off she went again, with her shawl tied around the pot, dragging it along behind her.

It wasn't long before she had to stop and rest again. She went to look at the silver in the pot, and found it wasn't a pot at all, but a solid lump of iron.

"Well!" said the old woman. "I do get luckier and luckier still!

I'd never have known what to do with all that silver, for I've never had more than one silver sixpence at a time in all my life before. But a lump of iron is just what I've been needing to prop my door open, so that the sun can shine straight in."

Off she went again, with her shawl wrapped around the lump of iron, dragging it behind her. She didn't stop until she came to her own front door.

Then she bent down to untie the shawl. As soon as she had, the lump of iron shook itself, stood up on four long legs, gave a laugh, and went galloping off into the dark.

"Well!" said the old woman. "Isn't that the luckiest thing of all! If I hadn't brought home that old iron pot – that turned out to be full of gold – that turned out to be silver – that turned out to be a lump of iron – I'd never have seen the Hedley Kow with these two eyes of mine. I must be the luckiest old woman alive."

The Great Rain

A Native American legend

•

 Linda Cotterill

It was very strange weather. Purple and black clouds raced and tumbled across the sky. They hid the sun; they hid the mountain tops. Inside the clouds, lightning flashed and thunder rumbled. Nokomis, the Great Earth Spirit, watched the sky and was worried.

"This isn't the right weather for summer," she thought. "Why is the Thunderbird making it so dark and stormy? Thunderbird!" she called. "What's wrong?"

"Kaaa!" screeched a voice inside the clouds. "I'll tell you what's wrong! I'm angry!"

There was a flash of lightning, and the clouds tore apart.

Nokomis could see the Thunderbird crouching over the mountains, his talons gripping their tops, his open wings stretching from horizon to horizon.

"Very angry!" he shouted, and lightning darted from his red eyes.

"But why are you angry?" asked Nokomis.

"Why?" He glared down at her, stretching his neck and rattling his wings to send thunder rolling about the sky.

"I'm angry because the people love you and they don't love me!"

"They love me because I'm the earth, their home," Nokomis said. "I'm the rivers where they fish, the forests where they hunt, and the plains where they pitch their teepees. They dance and give thanks to you for the rain you send," she reminded him.

"But they love you best!" He beat his wings until the thunder shook the mountainside.

"I'll show them. I'll send them so much rain that the rivers will flood and cover their forests and their plains and their teepees. Everyone will drown. Then they'll be sorry! Kaaa!" He screamed, stretching wide his eagle beak, then pulled the black clouds over himself again.

"Thunderbird, Thunderbird," called Nokomis, but he would not answer.

Nokomis was very worried. "What am I going to do?" she thought. "He won't talk to me. And he won't change his mind. I know him. He'll just sulk up there getting angrier and angrier until he's ready to burst. Then he'll do what he said – make it rain and rain."

She looked at the mountain where Thunderbird was hiding and thought hard.

"I don't think he can make enough rain to cover everything. Not everything. Not the mountains. Yes! That's it!"

Nokomis called. "Listen to me, all you animals and people, there is going to be a terrible flood. You must go high up in the mountains; you'll be safe there. You must go quickly."

Her voice traveled everywhere. In the grass, jackrabbits heard her and stopped nibbling. Beneath the ground, moles heard her and stopped digging. Under the water, beavers heard her and stopped building their dams. Soon all the animals and insects were flying, running, and hopping to the mountains.

It was only the people who took no notice. In their villages, they went on sewing moccasins, making arrows, and looking at the sky.

"It's too noisy in those villages – everyone talking – they can't hear me," Nokomis thought. "I must find someone quiet to tell."

In the long grass, she saw a boy looking for rabbits. Not a twig snapped, not a blade of grass squeaked as he crept forward, an arrow ready in his bow.

"It's Blue Jay," smiled Nokomis. "He's as silent as a shadow, he'll hear me. Blue Jay! Blue Jay!" she called, but he didn't seem to hear. He went on quietly slipping through the grass. Nokomis called louder, "Blue Jay, you must tell your family and everyone to go into the mountains."

But Blue Jay thought her voice was only the sound of the wind.

"How noisy the wind is today – shaking the trees and rattling the bushes. It will frighten away all the rabbits," he thought and carried on hunting.

"How deaf these humans are!" said Nokomis. "Who else can I tell?"

By the river, she saw a girl. With her fish-spear ready, she crouched barefoot on a rock. She was waiting for a speckled trout to come out of the weeds.

"It's Little Otter," smiled Nokomis. "She's as silent as that rock – she'll hear me."

Just to make sure this time she called very loudly, "Little Otter, Little Otter!"

But Little Otter took no notice. She had seen the shadow of a fish. Holding her breath, she leaned forward and lifted her spear above her head. She stared hard into the water and didn't look around.

"Little Otter!" Nokomis called again. "You must listen to me – there isn't much time – listen to me – Little Otter – listen to me!" But Little Otter thought her voice was only the sound of the river.

"How noisy the water is today, clattering and chattering over the stones. It will frighten away all the fish," she thought and carried on fishing.

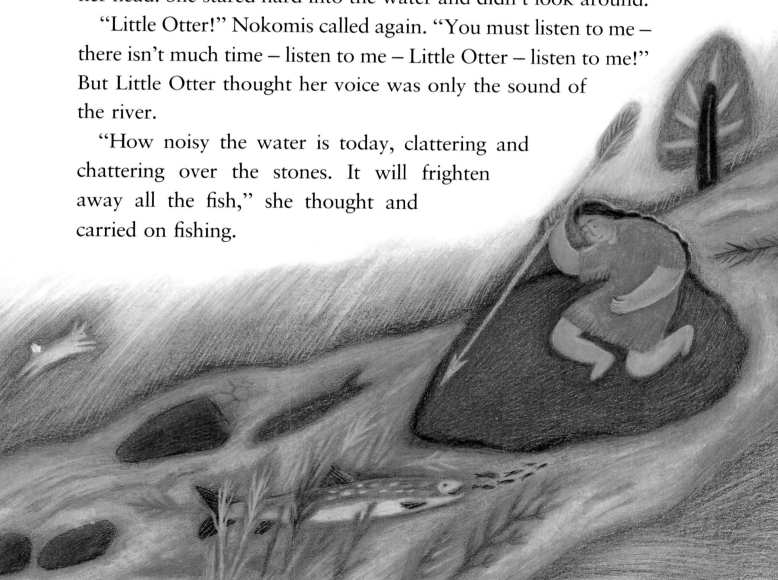

Nokomis was puzzled. "These humans only seem to understand their own language. I must find some other way to warn them, something they will understand."

She frowned up at the sky. It was much darker, and behind the clouds thunder muttered. Soon the Thunderbird would start the rain.

A little while later, an old woman strode into the village where Blue Jay and Little Otter lived. She was tall and thin. Her face and hands were wrinkled like bark. She wore a dress of soft green buckskin with fringe down the sleeves and brown moccasins embroidered with flowers. Her gray hair hung in a long braid and in her headband was one eagle feather dyed red.

Gathering all the people around her she said, "The Thunderbird is very angry. He is going to make so much rain that all this land will be covered with water. If you stay here, you'll drown; but in the mountains, you'll be safe."

No one in the village had seen the old woman before, but her face and eyes were very old and very wise so they believed her. They folded their teepees, stamped out their cooking fires, packed pots and blankets and babies into carrying baskets, and went into the mountains.

All that day, the old woman hurried from village to village warning people. Soon almost all the people were safe in the mountains. There was only one village left to tell.

As the old woman came near, she heard drumming and singing. The people were having a feast. In the center of the teepees, people were dancing, stamping their feet, and jumping high into the air. Some had drums, and others had rattles made from dried seed pods and shells tied on sticks. The noise was louder than the thunder.

No one noticed the old woman come into the village. She called to the dancers, "Listen to me, people!" but they danced on. "If those drums stopped, they could hear me," she said, but the drummers said, "This is dancing time, Grandma," and drummed louder.

"Maybe just one person will listen," she thought. She tried to grab a man dancing by. He pulled his arm away and yelled at her, "Leave me alone, old woman! Can't you see I'm dancing!"

The old woman was getting angry. She pushed her way through the dancers. She was very strong for such an old woman. She stood in the center of the dancers and shouted.

"A terrible storm is coming. The water will cover the tops of the tallest trees."

The people only laughed. "That will be very wet indeed, old woman! You had better run away quickly, or you will be drowned."

"If you don't go to the mountains, it is you who will be drowned," said the old woman. "Look at the sky; see how angry the Thunderbird is."

The sky was full of red and black clouds.

"How does an old woman like you know what the Thunderbird is feeling? Go away!" they shouted. "You are spoiling our dancing."

They made a circle and twisted and turned around her, singing and laughing. When she tried to speak again, they shook their rattles at her. They pushed her and bumped her.

They were making so much noise that they didn't hear the Thunderbird leap into the air and fly.

"Kaaa!" he screamed. "Kaaa!"

When thunder boomed and roared from his wings, they only shook their rattles and shouted louder than ever.

When the lightning crackled and jumped, they leaped higher and shouted, "See! See! The lightning is dancing with us!"

Even when the rain began to fall, faster and faster, in bigger and bigger drops, they only danced, wilder than ever. They whirled and pranced, spinning and kicking.

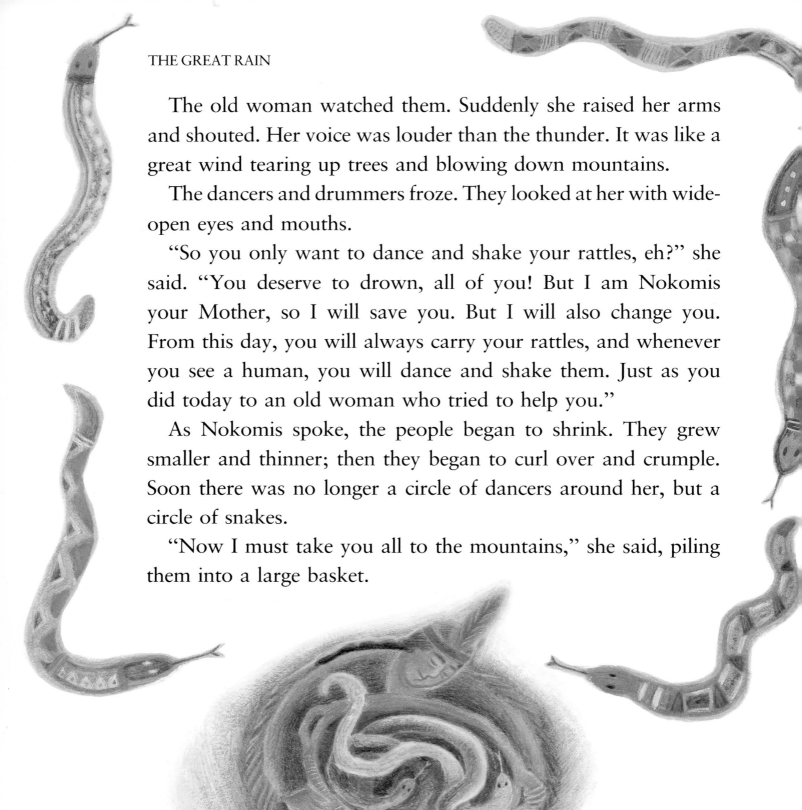

The old woman watched them. Suddenly she raised her arms and shouted. Her voice was louder than the thunder. It was like a great wind tearing up trees and blowing down mountains.

The dancers and drummers froze. They looked at her with wide-open eyes and mouths.

"So you only want to dance and shake your rattles, eh?" she said. "You deserve to drown, all of you! But I am Nokomis your Mother, so I will save you. But I will also change you. From this day, you will always carry your rattles, and whenever you see a human, you will dance and shake them. Just as you did today to an old woman who tried to help you."

As Nokomis spoke, the people began to shrink. They grew smaller and thinner; then they began to curl over and crumple. Soon there was no longer a circle of dancers around her, but a circle of snakes.

"Now I must take you all to the mountains," she said, piling them into a large basket.

It rained for days and weeks. Just as the Thunderbird had threatened, the forest and the plains were covered with water. But up in the mountains, the animals and people were safe.

When the rain stopped, the water drained away. Soon everybody went back to their homes.

Including the snakes. They went far away from rain and lived in dry places. And whenever they see a human, they raise their heads, sway as if they were dancing, and shake their rattles which they carry in their tails.

And that is how Nokomis the Great Earth Spirit brought rattlesnakes into the world.